MICHAEL DAHL'S
REALLY SCARY STORIES

Michael Dahl's Really Scary Stories
are published by Stone Arch Books,
A Capstone Imprint
1710 Roe Crest Drive
North Mankato, Minnesota 56003
www.capstonepub.com

Library of Congress Cataloging-in-Publication Data
Dahl, Michael, author.
   The doll that waved goodbye : and other scary tales / by Michael
Dahl ; illustrated by Xavier Bonet.
         pages cm. -- (Michael Dahl's really scary stories)
   Summary: Livia wears a small porcelain hand around her neck, all
that is left of a doll that once belonged to her grandmother, but on
the first night at summer camp the hand comes alive and terrifies
an envious cabinmate--and there are plenty of chills in five other
stories in this collection.
   ISBN 978-1-4965-0595-8 (library binding) -- ISBN 978-1-4965-2333-4
(ebook pdf)
1. Dolls--Juvenile fiction. 2. Horror tales. [1. Horror stories. 2.
Short stories.] I. Bonet, Xavier, 1979- illustrator. II. Title.
   PZ7.D15134Do 2016
   813.54--dc23
   [Fic]

                                                      2015000126

Designer: Hilary Wacholz
Image Credits: Dmitry Natashin

Printed in China by Nordica.
0415/CA21500548
032015   008842NORDF15

THE DOLL THAT WAVED GOODBYE

AND OTHER SCARY TALES

By Michael Dahl

Illustrated by
Xavier Bonet

STONE ARCH BOOKS
a capstone imprint

TABLE OF CONTENTS

Dear Reader,

I LIVE IN A HAUNTED HOUSE.

Not everyone believes me, but I've seen the ghost. Her name is Helen. One night I stood at the end of my hallway and saw Helen glide into my bedroom.

That's the only word for it. *Glide.*

I slept on the couch that night.

The previous owners told me Helen's name. They did not tell me what she looked like. I found that out for myself.

It seems we all find out what scares us when we are alone.

Now it's your turn to be alone. Alone with this book. Just you and the pages and the stories. You'll find out what scares the people in the stories.

At the same time, you might also find out what scares you . . .

Michael Dahl

ONE HUNDRED HUNDRED WORDS

Nobody believes me. But I still have to tell someone, anyone. You. Whoever is reading this,

PLEASE READ CAREFULLY.

Our brains are falling apart.

Doctors don't know what to call it. Kids call it "Zombie Creep." It started in Iceland. Now it's everywhere. You get it from breathing the same air as a sick person. Your brain gets smaller and smaller. You can tell you have it because it rots your thinking. Your words.

Soon you can only use a few words at a time. Only a hundred each day! But there's a cure. All you have to do is

DON'T LET THE BEDBUG BITE

"**B**edbug! Bedbug!" shouted the little boy.

"That's just Norman's way of saying he doesn't want to go to bed," his mother, Mrs. Brocken, explained to the babysitter.

"Bedbug!" Norman said again.

"He's been saying that ever since the other night," said Mrs. Brocken. "My husband told him, 'Good night, sleep tight, don't let the bedbugs bite.'"

"Bite! Bite!" said Norman.

"You can ignore him, Cleo," Mrs. Brocken said. "Put him to bed right at eight o'clock."

Norman sobbed.

Cleo Henderson babysat for all the families in the neighborhood. This was the first time she had been hired by the Brockens.

Norman was cute. He had curly red hair and bright-blue eyes. But now his eyes were filling up with tears. Baby tears. And Cleo hated baby tears. She felt helpless whenever she saw them. She knew that being the babysitter meant that she was in charge. But baby tears always got to her.

"Maybe we can stay up and read a story if he has trouble sleeping?" asked Cleo, looking at Mrs. Brocken.

"Bedtime is eight o'clock," said Mrs. Brocken firmly. She stepped into her fancy shoes and checked her hair in the hallway mirror. Then Mr. Brocken came down the stairs. He was wearing a nice suit and tie.

Mr. Brocken looked at his crying child. "Don't tell me," he said. "Bedbugs?"

"I don't know why you ever said that to him," said Mrs. Brocken.

"Everybody says it," snapped Mr. Brocken. "It doesn't mean anything."

"Bedbug! Bedbug!" yelled the red-faced Norman.

"Does he think there are real bugs in his bed?" asked Cleo. She could understand Norman's terror if he had seen an actual bug in his bed. Cleo hated bugs, too. She hated all creepy-crawly things.

"Who knows what's going on in his little brain," Mrs. Brocken said, picking up her purse.

"Bite! Bite!" screamed Norman.

Mr. Brocken threw up his arms. "That's enough, Norman!" he shouted.

Both Cleo and Norman were surprised. Norman even stopped crying.

"I'm going up there right now to prove that there are no — I repeat *no* — bedbugs!" Mr. Brocken continued. "And then you are going to bed!" He angrily marched up the stairs, and Cleo heard a door bang shut.

The house was totally quiet. Then Mrs. Brocken said, "See, Norman? See what you've done? You made your daddy really mad and ruined —"

Suddenly, a terrible scream came from upstairs. It came from Norman's room.

Mrs. Brocken raced upstairs, followed closely by Cleo, who held onto Norman's hand.

When they opened the bedroom door, they found Mr. Brocken lying quietly on Norman's bed. He looked like he was fast asleep.

"What are you doing?" asked Mrs. Brocken. "Why did you scream?"

Mr. Brocken didn't answer. He didn't move.

But the pillow under his head moved. A hairy black arm, about seven feet long, crept out from under the pillow. Then a second arm reached out from the other side.

Two see-through wings, like giant tennis rackets, sprung up on either side of the mattress. The legs of the bed began to shake. A loud hum filled the air.

Cleo couldn't look away from the horrible scene. Mrs. Brocken screamed. The giant bug was shaking so much now that Mr. Brocken's shoes came off his feet and slid across the bug's smooth, inky shell and down to the bedroom floor.

Then the wings flapped. The bedbug scurried over to the open bedroom window, put its long front feelers on the sill, and leaped into the air. The awful creature flew around the Brockens' backyard. Mr. Brocken still lay quietly, as if glued to the bug's back. With a loud buzz, the bug flew above the roof and was lost in the starry night sky.

"Bedbug! Bedbug!" said Norman.

Cleo hugged the little boy. He squirmed in her arms and pointed, but not at the window this time. He pointed toward a dark corner of the bedroom. Cleo saw five or six large white shapes, as round as basketballs, nestled in the corner.

They were eggs. And their shells were starting to crack.

PICKLED

It was Tom's idea to take the shortcut home on the last day of school.

Gus, Raymond, and I followed him out of the school building, past the buses, past the screaming kids. He led us into the woods behind the school. It was faster than walking through the neighborhood and much cooler than taking the bus.

We had heard stories about the woods. Grown-ups said there had been a farm there years ago. A tornado had ripped through the town, across the fields, and swept up the farmer, his family, and his entire house. There was nothing left but a few lost pigs and a cow.

Trees and weeds took over the abandoned fields. No one ever moved in.

Now kids said the woods were haunted.

As we walked through the trees, pushing branches out of the way, Gus said, "I bet this place is haunted." He was always saying the obvious.

"Watch out for the bloody farmer," Tom called from up ahead. "He hides up in the trees, waiting for a victim."

"To eat?" asked Gus.

"That reminds me," I said. "I still have some lunch left. Anyone want a pickle?"

No one was hungry.

Tom and Raymond went ahead to explore, while Gus and I walked slowly.

The woods were thicker than I'd expected. Darker, too. We all froze when Raymond suddenly shouted, "You guys! Come quick!"

He was standing in a small clearing up ahead, pointing at the ground. He had a rip in his jeans and dirt all over his face.

"You have dirt all over your face," said Gus.

"I know, I know," said Raymond. "Look what I tripped over."

He pointed to a flat piece of wood in the dirt. A rusty metal handle stuck out of it. It looked like part of an old door.

"The door to the old farmer's house," whispered Tom.

"The house that was wrecked by the tornado?" asked Gus.

Raymond stood over the metal handle and kicked away some dirt with his shoe. "It's bigger," he said. We all joined in, digging and kicking at the dirt. After a minute we had uncovered the whole door.

Tom knelt down and looked hard at the handle. Underneath it was a small, round keyhole. Tom put his face close to the keyhole. He glanced up at me with a funny look.

"Garvey," he whispered. He always called me by my last name. "Put your hand over this."

I bent down and held out my hand. I felt a cool stream of air escape from the rusty keyhole.

Tom stood up. "This ain't just a door," he said. "I mean, this is a *real* door. A door with something behind it."

"It's a storm shelter," said Gus. We all stared at him. None of us had heard Gus actually come up with an idea before. "Where you hide from a tornado," he explained. "My great-grandma has one under her house."

A shelter. Where the farmer and his family hid during the storm years ago. We were all thinking the same thing. No one wanted to say it out loud. *Dead bodies.*

"Or it could be a root cellar," Gus said. "My great-grandma puts stuff in jars and keeps them in a different cellar."

"Preserves," said Raymond.

Gus nodded. "Like pickles and apples and jelly and stuff."

"Or maybe," said Tom, "it's buried treasure." He leaned down, gripped the handle, and pulled open the door. We all stepped back.

A wave of cool air rushed up out of the hole. Old wooden steps led down into darkness.

"It's dark down there," said Gus.

"Who wants to go first?" Raymond asked. No one spoke.

"Tom opened it," I said.

"Garvey's not scared," Tom said, still holding the door. "He'll go."

I nodded but didn't say anything. Now I had to go.

I walked to the top of the steps. It was impossible to see anything down there. I took a step down.

"See anything?" asked Gus.

"I'm not even down there yet," I said.

I took a few more steps. It was still too dark to see. It felt cooler.

The smell wasn't bad. It reminded me of how the grass smells after my dad mows the lawn. But there was another smell, too. It smelled like there might be animals down here.

My eyes were getting used to the darkness. I heard something squeak.

"Any treasure?" Gus called from above.

I heard a hiss from below. Then a word. "Ssssafe," I thought it said.

I was so scared, I was barely able to talk. "Wh-who's there?" I said.

"Is it . . . safe?" came the voice.

Someone lit a match, and the light from it blinded me. I saw a candle in midair. Then I saw the hand holding it. A hand that was wrinkly and covered in dirt. It had black fingernails curved like claws.

"Is the tornado gone?" asked another higher voice.

Four shadows stood in front of me. It looked like a family. A husband and wife and two children. When my eyes got used to the light, I saw that their skin hung off their bones. I had seen a mummy once on a school field trip to the museum. Their four faces looked like that. Sunken eyes. Hollow cheeks.

"That tornado's bad," said the man.

"Good thing we have this shelter," said the woman.

"Good thing we have some food down here, too," said the man. "How bad is it out there, son?" he asked.

I tried to take a step back, but the stair I was standing on broke, and I fell. "Help!" I shouted.

I heard Gus scream from above. Tom yelled a curse word and let go of the door. It dropped with a bang, and the *whoosh* of air made the candle blow out.

"Help!" I cried again. I could hear my friends shouting to each other as they ran away. I tried backing up the stairs, but they rotted and crumbled into dust. The door was too high to reach. I couldn't see a thing.

"You're safe from the storm down here," said the farmer.

"We'll stay here till it's all over," said the farmer's wife.

I heard them coming closer. It sounded like their bodies were dragging across the dirt floor.

There was another voice, quiet and mumbly. I was only able to make out a single word. "Hungry . . . hungry . . ."

The dragging sound came again from the dirt floor.

"Mumummm . . . hungry . . . ?"

The voice sounded much closer. It was the boy. The farmer's son. *Was he going to eat me?*

I heard shuffling and then the sound of metal grind against glass. A lid was being unscrewed. Then I heard the voice again. The boy's mouth was next to my ear. I could feel his warm, stinky breath.

"Are you hungry?" said the boy. "Want a pickle?"

DEAD END

Ren was riding his bicycle late one afternoon when he saw the sign:

LOSA STREET

And under that:

DEAD END

Never saw that one, he thought.

New houses were going up all the time in his neighborhood. New houses needed new streets. And new streets were new adventures. Ren turned his bike onto the new road and pedaled faster.

He counted twenty or so empty, new houses along the way to the dead end. His dad had a fancy word for this kind of dead end — *cul-de-sac*. In fact, Ren's family lived on a cul-de-sac. Their house was bunched up with four others around a wide, paved circle.

Ren loved to ride his bicycle around the circles — especially when he discovered a new one. When he reached the end of Losa Street, he shot around it several times without holding onto the handlebars. He felt like he was flying. Like he had wings.

Buffalo chicken wings! he thought.

His mom was making wings for dinner tonight. His favorite. Ren broke out of his circling pattern and headed back, counting the houses as he went.

He counted up to thirty. *Where is that sign?* Ren wondered. *Shouldn't I be at the end of the street by now?*

The street curved back and forth without coming to an end. Ren braked suddenly. The road had led him to another cul-de-sac. He must have missed the turn-off.

Ren headed back, and this time he pedaled harder. The late afternoon sun was setting behind the empty houses. He saw for the first time that all the houses sat behind high chain-link fences. The gates at the end of their driveways had large metal locks holding them closed. The builders probably were trying to keep curious kids away from the half-finished homes.

Ren slowed down. He couldn't believe it. He was at another cul-de-sac! It looked exactly like first one he had visited. No . . . it *was* the first! He remembered seeing those two pink houses next to each other, with the creepy troll statue in between them. How could he have missed the turn-off a second time?

Even though the air was cool, Ren was sweating. He circled the dead end and biked back the way he'd come. This time, he rode slower.

He saw that the addresses started at 40. So he counted the houses along the way as carefully as he could. Ren knew that the addresses should get lower as he got closer to the entrance to the street.

Where is the sign that says Losa Street? he wondered.

Finally, Ren saw it. The back of the sign. He rode closer. *Wait a second . . .* Ren thought. It was the other sign. *DEAD END.* And that's exactly what he found beyond it. The other cul-de-sac.

It didn't make sense. A street with two dead ends?

He had been counting the houses. Reading the shiny new address numbers nailed beside each door. The numbers got lower . . . 17 . . . 13 . . . 11 . . . 9 . . . 5 . . . then they stopped. And there was the dead end.

But wait! Ren pedaled down the street the other way again, counting the numbers as they got higher. As he pedaled, he saw that the highest address was 37. But Ren was sure that last time he'd pedaled here, the houses had started at 40.

Ren began to worry. He rode back again, counting the numbers out loud.

This time, 5 and 9 were gone.

What's going on? Houses are vanishing . . . Ren thought.

The street was getting shorter. The sun was moving lower in the sky behind the row of empty buildings.

"Hey!" Ren yelled. His voice echoed along the street.

He thought he heard dogs barking. Ren followed the sound, but it only led him back to the first cul-de-sac. And he didn't come across any dogs there.

Maybe I'm dreaming, Ren thought. *Maybe I fell off my bike and hit my head. That's it! I must be imagining things. If I get off my bike, walk, and take some deep breaths, I'll feel better.*

He hopped off his bike and began to walk back and forth slowly on the dark street, holding onto the handlebars of his bike. *In real life,* Ren thought, *every street has a beginning and end. It has to. Otherwise, how would people get home?*

When Ren felt a little better, he looked up ahead again. But what he saw was the thing he most feared.

The street was so short that he could see both cul-de-sacs. They were facing each other. The street was getting narrower, too. The fences on both sides were closer.

Ren wiped the sweat off his forehead and blinked. When he opened his eyes, there was no longer a street . . . only one dead end. A high chain-link fence surrounded him. He felt like a bird trapped in a cage.

Ren dropped his bike onto the asphalt. He ran up to one of the locked gates and shook it. "Hey!" he yelled at the house on the other side. "Hey, someone! Is there someone there?"

The windows of the house stared back at him like black, empty eyes.

"Hello? Anyone?" he called.

Ren thought about climbing the fence. But he looked up and saw there was barbed wire at the top. Plus, he felt so tired.

Ren turned and walked back to his bike. His bike? It was gone.

He stood alone inside the circle, inside the fence.

Ren looked up. The sunlight was fading. His strength was fading, too. The last ray of sunlight hit a sign hanging on the fence. It was the sign he had seen when he first turned onto Losa Street. *DEAD END*. He was sure it was the same sign.

Except now, one of the words was gone.

MEET THE
PARENTS

Matt Rooney sat on the sofa in the living room. He stared across the room at his favorite photo on the wall. In it, he and his parents were each holding a pair of skis. All three of them were smiling at the camera. A snowy mountain sat in the background. They had been so happy on that trip.

Tonight was different. No one was happy. And Matt was afraid. He kept looking away from his parents as they spoke to him from across the coffee table.

"Before your real parents get here, there's something you should know," said his father.

"You're going to scare him," Mrs. Rooney whispered to her husband.

"I heard that!" said Matt. "What do you mean, 'scare' me?"

Mr. Rooney cleared his throat and started over. "As I said, uh, before your real parents get here —"

"But *you're* my real parents!" shouted Matt. "I don't care that I'm adopted!"

Matt's mom sighed, her eyes watery and tired. She leaned on her husband.

"Your *natural* parents, I mean," his dad said.

"I don't want to go with them," cried Matt.

Matt's mom sat down next to him on the sofa. "You don't *have* to do anything, Mattie," she replied. "But they wrote and asked to see you, so —"

"Well, I don't want to see them," said Matt. "And you still didn't tell me what was going to scare me."

His dad looked quickly at his mother. "Well, sometimes families have problems," he said.

"Your natural mother and father had to go away for a time," added his mom. "They had no choice. And they needed someone to take care of their special baby."

"Special?" Matt asked. "Is something wrong with me?"

"There's absolutely nothing wrong with you," his dad said. "You know that." He sat down on the other side of Matt, putting his hand on his son's shoulder.

"You mean my back, don't you?" asked Matt. Matt had been born with his back covered in thick, bumpy skin. It didn't look pretty in the mirror, but Matt was used to it by now. It never stopped him from joining activities. He wore a T-shirt whenever he went swimming, but that was the only thing he did differently from his friends.

"No, I don't mean your back," said his father.

A *thud* shook the house, and Matt's dad stood up.

"What was that?" Matt said. He turned and looked out the living room window.

It was evening. Their house sat at the bend of a sharp curve. The street trailed off into darkness on either side. Two or three streetlights stretched overhead like dinosaur necks.

Thud! The windows rattled.

"Oh, honey," said Matt's mother as she jumped from the sofa and grabbed her husband's hands.

"It's them," said his father.

Thud!

"Them? Them who?" asked Matt. His father didn't answer. Instead, he went to the front door and opened it.

"Mom, who is Dad talking about?" Matt asked. His mother joined her husband at the door. They both stood there, holding hands, silently staring outside.

"*Now* you're scaring me," said Matt.

The *thuds* grew louder. Matt leaned over the back of the sofa and peered out the window.

A shadow stood in the middle of the street. It was blocks away, but even at that distance

Matt could tell the creature was huge. The head of the thing almost touched the streetlights. A second slightly smaller shadow appeared behind it.

The two shadows moved forward on legs as thick as tree trunks.

"What . . . is that?" Matt asked weakly.

"Them," said his mother.

"Them who?" Matt cried again. He saw the two shadows reach out and hold hands. His head hurt. "You don't mean those — things — are . . . are . . ." He couldn't finish the sentence.

The shadows marched toward the house. They smashed through the bushes at the end of the driveway. They knocked branches off the tree in the front yard. Cracks appeared in the living room window with each new *thud*.

As the creatures came closer, an awful smell became stronger and stronger. *What is that terrible smell?* Matt wondered. It made him think of vomit on a pile of wet leaves.

A groan rumbled through the house like a thunderstorm.

His mom said in a tiny voice, "Mattie, honey, someone's asking to meet you."

Matt felt sick, but he managed to make it to the doorway without throwing up. The creatures were covered in long, droopy, vine-like stuff. *Is that their fur?* he wondered. They were walking lumps of grass. Matt saw bugs crawling over them.

The taller creature let out an ear-ringing roar. "MATT!!!"

Matt gulped. He grabbed for his mom's hand. Then he gulped again. Then he said, "Are . . . are you my . . . parents?"

The huge creatures began to shiver. The odor got worse. A swarm of bugs flew off the vines and buzzed into the house.

"I think they're laughing," said Matt's dad.

"What's so funny?" asked Matt.

The bigger one spoke. "No," boomed the deep voice. "Not your parents."

Matt sighed. *My parents aren't monsters after all,* he thought.

The second giant said, "We are servants. Work for your parents. Here they are."

A cry pierced the night air. Two strange figures soared over the treetops. They sailed above the streetlights and dove toward the ground. Graceful as eagles, they landed on the front lawn and walked to the front door on slender legs.

"Mattie!" said the female. "My baby!" The beautiful woman looked human except for the pale, bat-like wings on her back. She knelt and gave Matt a hug.

The man stood up straight and proud and shook hands with Matt's dad. "Thank you for taking care of him," he said. "We are sorry we haven't been here. But now we are allowed to visit your world for short periods of time."

"I hope you don't mind if we take Mattie for the weekend?" said the female.

Matt's mom smiled. "Of course not. Um, would you like some coffee?"

Matt couldn't speak. What was happening? His T-shirt felt tight on his body. His back stung and burned. Then he heard a ripping sound.

He stumbled, gripping the side of the door for balance. All of a sudden he felt light as air.

The strange man smiled down at Matt. "Yes, my son," he said. "You have wings."

The two grassy creatures were ordered to gather up Matt's bedroom furniture and all his clothes and video games and soccer ball and books — because he wasn't sure what he'd need over the next few days. Far above them soared the reunited family.

Matt was still afraid, but his fear had changed. At the beginning of the evening, he had been afraid of who, or what, his parents might be.

Now, he was afraid of falling. He had never used wings before. He had never known he had them, folded under his bumpy back. As the cool air rushed past his face, though, he found his balance. He stretched out his arms, leaning into the wind. He was sure he would get the hang of it. It reminded him of skiing.

THE DOLL
THAT WAVED
GOODBYE

Livia wore a doll's hand around her neck.

The doll had first belonged to Livia's grandmother. She had passed it down to Livia's mother, who had then given it to Livia. Over the years, the doll's green silk dress had grown worn and tattered. It had lost an arm when Livia's mother and aunt fought over the doll as children. Livia's cat had scratched the head and ripped off its real human hair that was tied in tiny braids. Piece by piece, the little doll had fallen apart. Finally, only the left hand remained, and Livia now wore it as a necklace.

Livia had explained this to the other girls on her first night at summer camp. The girls in her cabin were getting ready for bed when one of them, Emily, saw something moving at Livia's throat. It was the hand, swinging on its chain.

The girls all looked closer at the little hand.

"It's porcelain," Livia said.

"That's what my grandma's teacups are made of," said another girl, Amber.

Livia nodded. "It's very delicate."

All the girls could see that the little hand had tiny cracks running through it. The fingernails had faded from red to pink. A thin bracelet of gold wire wrapped around the doll's wrist. Another wire with a little hoop on the end stuck out of the wrist like a skinny bone. A chain ran through the hoop and hooked around Livia's neck.

Her cabin mates "oohed" and "ahhed" over the doll hand. A few of them asked to touch the white fingers, but Livia shook her head. "I'm sorry," she said. "But it's quite delicate. It's so old. And I'm so afraid it might break."

All of the girls understood. All except for Brooke.

Why can't I touch the doll hand? Brooke wondered as she sat in bed that night. *Just touching it once won't hurt.*

All night, while the others slept soundly in their bunks, Brooke stared at the bunk above hers. She was angry with Livia. Brooke hated snobby people, and she thought Livia was one of the worst. *So scared of letting anyone touch her stupid, precious doll,* thought Brooke. *Not even a doll. Only a stupid hand.*

But the more Brooke thought about it, the more she wanted to try on Livia's necklace. *Anyway, why shouldn't she touch it? Why not wear it?* It would only be for a minute. Half a minute. What was wrong with that?

But Brooke knew Livia would never give her permission, so she waited. All week she waited to find the necklace lying on the little table next to Livia's bunk. Or on her pillow. As the days rolled by at camp, however, Brooke learned that Livia never took off the doll hand. She wore it in the morning to the Sing-Fest. She wore it during crafting class. She wore it on the bird-watching hike. When the rest of the campers went swimming in the lake, Livia sat on the shore and read. She said the water could ruin the porcelain.

Every night as Livia got ready for bed, Brooke saw her pat the doll hand to make sure it was still there before she slipped into her bed to sleep.

Brooke grew angrier and angrier. *Who does Livia think she is, anyway? People are supposed to share. They're supposed to take turns.*

It just wasn't fair, Brooke thought, that she couldn't hold the doll necklace in her hands. Or feel it around her neck.

Late one night, when everyone in the cabin was asleep, Brooke threw back the cover of her sleeping bag and crept out of her bunk. It only took a few steps to reach the side of Livia's bunk. Brooke stood there, looking down at the sleeping snobby girl. It was hard to see in the darkness of the cabin. She bent closer toward Livia's neck.

Brooke gasped. She covered her mouth with her hands, afraid the sound might wake the sleeping girl.

The chain hung around Livia's neck as it always did, but the doll hand was gone.

Goose bumps ran up and down the back of Brooke's neck. She hurried back to her bunk and squirmed into her sleeping bag. She shivered, even under the thick cover. Why did the sight of the bare necklace frighten her? Perhaps the hand had slipped off while Livia slept, and it was hidden under her hair or her T-shirt.

Brooke closed her eyes and tried to calm down.

That was close, she thought. If her gasp had woken up Livia, what would she have said? What excuse would she have made up?

Just then, Brooke heard a tiny sound on the side of her bed. A soft, metallic sound. *Zzzzz.* The sound grew slightly louder, closer. *Zzzzz.* It reminded Brooke of a zipper.

Someone — or something — was zipping up her sleeping bag.

Brooke forced herself to open her eyes. But no one was standing beside her bed. All the girls were sleeping in their bunks.

The zipping stopped, but another sound took its place. Scratching. She felt something small crawling down her sleeping bag toward the foot of the bunk. Brooke thought of mice and almost screamed, but then the crawling stopped.

She took a deep breath. The sound returned, coming from the post of the bunk. It climbed up the post to the bunk above her. It stopped for a moment, but then it moved again.

Brooke saw a tiny shadow moving on the underside of the bunk above her. A mouse? A moth?

The shadow grew wider, as if a tiny hand were spreading its fingers.

Suddenly, a white hand fell from above and landed on Brooke's mouth. Its cold fingers grew and grew. Soon it was as large as a human hand. The hand was covered in cracks with pale pink fingernails.

Worst of all, the hand was strong enough to keep anyone from hearing Brooke cry out.

* * *

"Brooke's gone!"

Livia and the other girls woke up the following morning to Emily's cry. They were surprised to see Brooke's belongings all packed up. Her sleeping bag was rolled up neatly and resting on the floor. A few minutes later, the camp counselor came in, followed by Brooke who picked up her suitcase and bag and left without saying a word.

On her way out the door, the camp counselor turned to the speechless campers and whispered, "I think Brooke misses home. She had a bad night." Then she quietly closed the door behind her.

"She didn't even say goodbye," said Amber.

"What do you think happened?" asked Emily.

Livia giggled softly. Too softly for the others to hear. She wasn't laughing because Brooke was leaving. She was laughing as if she was being tickled. As if something small and delicate was wiggling near her throat. As if something small was waving goodbye.

ABOUT THE AUTHOR

Michael Dahl, the author of the Library of Doom and Troll Hunters series, is an expert on fear. He is afraid of heights (but he still flies). He is afraid of small, enclosed spaces (but his house is crammed with over 3,000 books). He is afraid of ghosts (but that same house is haunted). He hopes that by writing about fear, he will eventually be able to overcome his own. So far it is not working. But he is afraid to stop. He claims that, if he had to, he would travel to Mount Doom in order to toss in a dangerous piece of jewelry. Even though he is afraid of volcanoes. And jewelry.

ABOUT THE ILLUSTRATOR

Xavier Bonet is an illustrator and comic-book artist who resides in Barcelona. Experienced in 2D illustration, he has worked as an animator and a background artist for several different production companies. He aims to create works full of color, texture, and sensation, using both traditional and digital tools. His work in children's literature is inspired by magic and fantasy as well as his passion for the art.

MICHAEL DAHL TELLS ALL

Readers often ask me where I get my ideas. To be honest, I don't always know! Sometimes the ideas arrive on the doorstep of my imagination all dressed up and say, "You were expecting us, right?" Other times they come in dreams, quietly and politely. Still others come when I brainstorm with friends, write down sentences in a notebook, or take a long walk. Here's where the stories in this book came from.

ONE HUNDRED WORDS

My friend Donnie gave me a challenge. "What if you only had one hundred words to tell a story?" he asked. "What if something terrible was happening to you, and you only had one hundred words to ask for help?" This short short story was my answer to that challenge.

DON'T LET THE BEDBUG BITE

You can't write scary stories without one of them being about a babysitter. I heard so many creepy tales growing up that involved babysitting — the house is unfamiliar, the grown-ups are gone, it's dark outside. These ingredients set the heart racing. My friend Beth has an amazing kid named Sam who once was afraid of bedbugs. Sam was sure he saw a bug in his bed. If I were Sam, I'd be afraid of bedbugs, too. I wondered, what if the bug wasn't in the bed, but *was* the bed?

PICKLED

Tornadoes are common in the Midwest. When I was in fifth grade, four of them jumped over my house. My family was lucky. Those same tornadoes ripped apart our town, carved craters in our streets, and damaged many lives. Which is why I still fear storms. I've sat in many basements waiting for storms to pass. But how long should a person wait to come out? I've read about soldiers who hid during World War II and didn't know the war was over until years later. In the dark, it's easy to lose track of time.

DEAD END

I was driving home from work and saw a Dead End sign. *Whoosh!* The whole story jumped into my brain. It probably has something to do with my fear of getting lost. See? I told you that lots of things scare me.

MEET THE PARENTS

When we were kids, my sisters and I often imagined that we were adopted. Our real parents, we believed, were rulers of some European kingdom, waiting to reclaim us. Waiting for us to return to a castle, riches, and an endless supply of books and ice cream. Well, what if our true parents were not wonderful, but horrible? Or even monstrous? What would that be like?

THE DOLL THAT WAVED GOODBYE

One of the most frightening TV shows I ever watched was about a girl whose doll changed places with her. They each took turns being the doll and being the owner. Another spooky story on the show *The Twilight Zone* had a doll that could talk and sneak around the house at night. Both dolls were very protective of their owners. Very. The location of my story was inspired by the many summers I spent as a kid at a camp in northern Minnesota.

GLOSSARY

babysitter (BAY-bee-SIT-ur) — someone who takes care of children when their parents aren't home

barbed wire (BARBD WIRE) — small, sharp spikes of twisted wire, usually on top of fences

creature (KREE-chur) — a living being, human or animal

cure (KYOOR) — a treatment that helps to end a sickness

goose bumps (GOOS BUHMPS) — tiny bumps that can appear on your skin when you're scared, cold, or excited

grind (GRINDE) — to rub against something

metallic (met-AL-ik) — seeming like metal

obvious (AHB-vee-uhss) — seen or understood easily

preserves (pri-ZURVS) — fruit that is canned and saved

scurried (SKUR-eed) — hurried; moved quickly

swept (SWEPT) — carried rapidly

tornado (tor-NAY-doh) — a violent windstorm that causes a lot of damage; appears as a dark, funnel-shaped cloud

victim (VIK-tuhm) — a person who is cheated, tricked, or made to suffer

wiggling (WIG-uhl-ing) — making short, quick movements

DISCUSSION QUESTIONS

1. In "Dead End," Ren gets lost in his own neighborhood. Have you ever gotten lost? Discuss how it made you feel.

2. In the story "Pickled," Garvey is trapped inside a tornado shelter with a family that has been hiding there for years. Garvey's friends run away, leaving him there alone. Discuss what you would've done if you had been there.

3. Norman is terrified of bedbugs in the story "Don't Let the Bedbug Bite." Talk about the things you're most afraid of.

WRITING PROMPTS

1. I wrote "One Hundred Words" with a challenge in mind. Respond to the prompt that I used to help me come up with the first story in this book:

    What if you only had one hundred words to tell a story? What if something terrible was happening to you, and you only had one hundred words to ask for help?

2. Imagine you are Livia in the story "The Doll that Waved Goodbye." Write a version of the story from Livia's point of view.

3. Monsters, like the ones in "Meet the Parents," often show up in scary stories. What kind of monster scares you the most? Is it a ghost? A zombie? A goblin? Or something in between? Write a paragraph describing the monster.

WHAT SCARES YOU?

FIND OUT WITH MICHAEL DAHL'S REALLY SCARY STORIES.

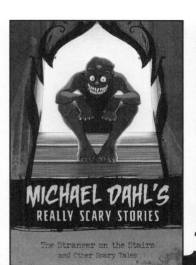

MICHAEL DAHL'S
REALLY SCARY STORIES

The Stranger on the Stairs
and Other Scary Tales

MICHAEL DAHL'S
REALLY SCARY STORIES

The Phantom on the Phone
and Other Scary Tales

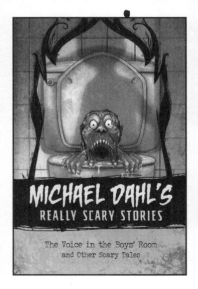

MICHAEL DAHL'S
REALLY SCARY STORIES

The Voice in the Boys' Room
and Other Scary Tales

MICHAEL DAHL'S
REALLY SCARY STORIES

The Doll that Waved Goodbye
and Other Scary Tales

MICHAEL DAHL'S
REALLY SCARY STORIES